Copyright © 1999 by Nord-Süd Verlag AG, Gossau Zürich, Switzerland.
First published in Switzerland under the title *Willst du mein Freund sein?*
English translation copyright © 1999 by North-South Books Inc.

First published in the United States, Great Britain, Canada, Australia, and New Zealand in 1999
by North-South Books, an imprint of Nord-Süd Verlag AG, Gossau Zürich, Switzerland.
First published in paperback in 2001 by North-South Books.
Distributed in the United States by North-South Books Inc., New York.

Library of Congress Cataloging-in-Publication Data
Krischanitz, Raoul.
[Willst du mein Freund sein? English]
Nobody likes me! / by Raoul Krischanitz; translated by Rosemary
Lanning.
        p.   cm.
"A Michael Neugebauer book."
Summary: When Buddy the dog tries to make friends with the other
animals he meets, it seems that none of them likes him until he
manages to clear up their confusion about him.
[1. Dogs—Fiction. 2. Animals—Fiction. 3. Friendship—Fiction.]
I. Lanning, Rosemary. II. Title.
PZ7.K8966No   1999
[E]—DC21   98-42106

A CIP catalogue record for this book is available from The British Library.

ISBN 0-7358-1054-0 (trade binding) 10 9 8 7 6 5 4 3 2 1
ISBN 0-7358-1055-9 (library binding) 10 9 8 7 6 5 4 3 2 1
ISBN 0-7358-1488-0 (paperback binding) 10 9 8 7 6 5 4 3 2 1
Printed in Belgium

For more information about our books, and the authors and artists
who create them, visit our web site: www.northsouth.com

Nobody Likes Me!

By Raoul Krischanitz
Translated by Rosemary Lanning

A Michael Neugebauer Book
NORTH-SOUTH BOOKS
New York / London

Buddy was the new dog in town. He sat outside his house with nothing to do. He was bored.

He saw a mouse peeking out of a hole in the wall.

"Will you play with me?" he asked.

"Not now," squeaked the mouse, and she scuttled back in her hole.

"She wasn't very friendly," said Buddy. "I guess she doesn't like me. Well then, I'll find another friend," he declared, and he walked away.

Buddy came to another house.
He saw three cats sitting in the window.
They all stared at Buddy.
"They certainly don't look friendly," he said.
"I don't think they like me."
So he walked on.

Buddy walked up a hill. He saw three rabbits playing tag.
The rabbits stopped their game. They looked at Buddy, twitched
their noses, and ran away.

"They weren't very friendly," said Buddy with a sigh.
"I don't think they like me either."
So he walked on.

Buddy walked to the edge of a green field with a fence all around it.
He saw a flock of fluffy white sheep.
The sheep bleated at him, then ran off and huddled together in the
far corner of the field.
"They don't seem friendly at all," said Buddy sadly.
"I'm sure they don't like me."
Again he walked on.

Buddy trudged slowly toward the woods.
Suddenly a big dog ran up to him and started barking.
"Bow wow!" he barked. "Bow wow wow!"
Buddy ran away as fast as he could.
"It's no use," Buddy said. "Nobody likes me!"
And he began to cry.

"Hello! Who are you?" a deep voice inquired.
Buddy looked up and saw a fox.
"I'm Buddy," he said.
"Why were you crying?" asked the fox.
"Because nobody likes me," Buddy replied.
"Why not?" said the fox.
"I don't know," said Buddy.
"Perhaps you should ask," said the fox.
"I'll come with you if you want."

So Buddy and the fox went to see the dog.
"Bow wow! Bow wow!" he barked.
"Why are you barking at me?" Buddy asked.
"Because you might steal my bone," said the dog.

"I'd never do that!" cried Buddy.
"I just want to be friends."
"Well, why didn't you say so
in the first place?" said the dog.
"I'd be glad to be your friend."
So Buddy and the fox
and the dog walked on.

They came to the field filled with sheep.

"Why did you bleat and run away from me?" asked Buddy.

"We were afraid you were going to herd us into the shearing pen," the sheep replied.

"I'd never do that!" cried Buddy. "I just want to be friends."

"Well, why didn't you say so in the first place?" said the sheep. "We'd be glad to be your friends."

So Buddy and the fox and the dog and the sheep walked on.

The rabbits had come out to play again, but when they saw Buddy
they ran and hid.
"Come back!" called Buddy. "Why are you running away?"
"Because you are a dog," they said. "And dogs chase rabbits."
"I'd never do that!" cried Buddy. "I just want to be friends."
"Well, why didn't you say so in the first place?" said the rabbits.
"We'd be glad to be your friends."
So Buddy and the fox and the dog and the sheep and the rabbits
walked on.

The friends came to the house where the three cats lived.
"Why did you stare at me before?" Buddy asked.
"We thought you would attack us," said the cats.
"I'd never do that!" said Buddy. "I just want to be friends."
"Well, why didn't you say so?" said the cats. "We'd be glad to be your friends."
So Buddy and the fox and the dog and the sheep and the rabbits and
the cats walked on.

At last they arrived at Buddy's house.
"Look how many friends I have found, Mousey!" he said.
"Tell me: Why wouldn't you play with me before?"
"Because I was baking a cake," said the mouse.
"Would you all like a piece?"

All the friends had a tiny piece of the mouse's cake.
Then they played happily together until the sun went down.